4.1.19

Dan + Noel,

Hope this book brings you both as much joy as it did to create.

Wishing you all the best,

Monte E. Lee

Print information available on the last page

Rev. date: 02/06/2017

To order additional copies of this book, contact:
Xlibris
1-888-795-4274
www.Xlibris.com
Orders@Xlibris.com

TAX A. DERMY'S

TALES OF THE FURRED THE FINNED & FEATHERED PRESENTS

THE HEADLESS DUCKLING

ILLUSTRATIONS BY:
MERTS E. LOC

This book is dedicated
to the power of the
imagination.

You must open your minds
to read between the lines
for not everything is always
as it seems.

Enjoy,

FOR
JUDITH &
HATHIE

WITH LOVE

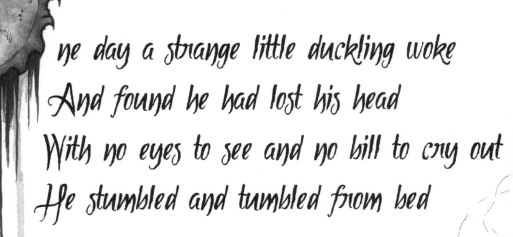

ne day a strange little duckling woke

And found he had lost his head

With no eyes to see and no bill to cry out

He stumbled and tumbled from bed

1

ut to the hallway and then down the stairs
The little duck tripped and stammered

Three steps more he found the front door
He kicked hard as his fuzzy wings hammered

ith a gust it swung wide

The fowl stepped outside

Not seeing the sun's glory

but he could feel it

He knew there and then he must have his head again

Or he'd find a better one and he'd steal it

Yes the plan was devine, a new skull he must find
And pluck it from the shoulders where it sits

Then on top of his stump
He'll place the new lump
And pray the fresh cranium fits

is new scheme in mind
The headless duckling set out to find
A better heading than he'd had once before

But with no sight to guide him
The road would not abide him
He had no hearing to warn him of dangers
And what's more...

9

e'd lost all his senses
So he caught
Himself in fences
Tripped on rocks and
Splashed through streams

11

umped his nub on low branches
And trotted through pig ranches
So maddening he wanted to scream

THWACK

e lept out at anything
    That had a head to take
  He even lept at several things
That had naught a head to make

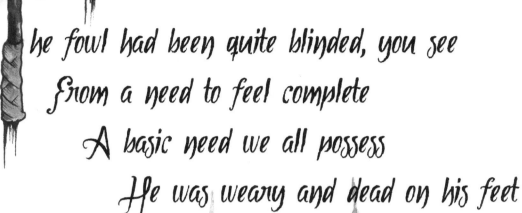

The fowl had been quite blinded, you see
From a need to feel complete
A basic need we all possess
He was weary and dead on his feet

He abandoned his plan of walking the land
and finding a head that would fit

If he could only remember where he'd put his
But he had neither brain to speak of nor whit

ouldn't curse couldn't frown
He just sat right down
Deciding to give up all together
But that my friends
Is when the duck's luck changed
When met by a fowl of a similar feather...

He heard not a sound

    Plopped fat on the ground

        But before him stood a figure most pleasant

All webby and downed and perfectly round

    It was no wildebeest, orangutan or pheasant

Fate as it seems had fulfilled the ducklings dreams

For a lady duckling crouched just before him

And she knew at first sight

She'd fill his days with delight

She would steer him from life's evils

And adore him

Because in the back of her mind
She'd been longing to find
A headless duckling in search of a head

And now she had found
Right here on the ground
The honey and jam to her bread

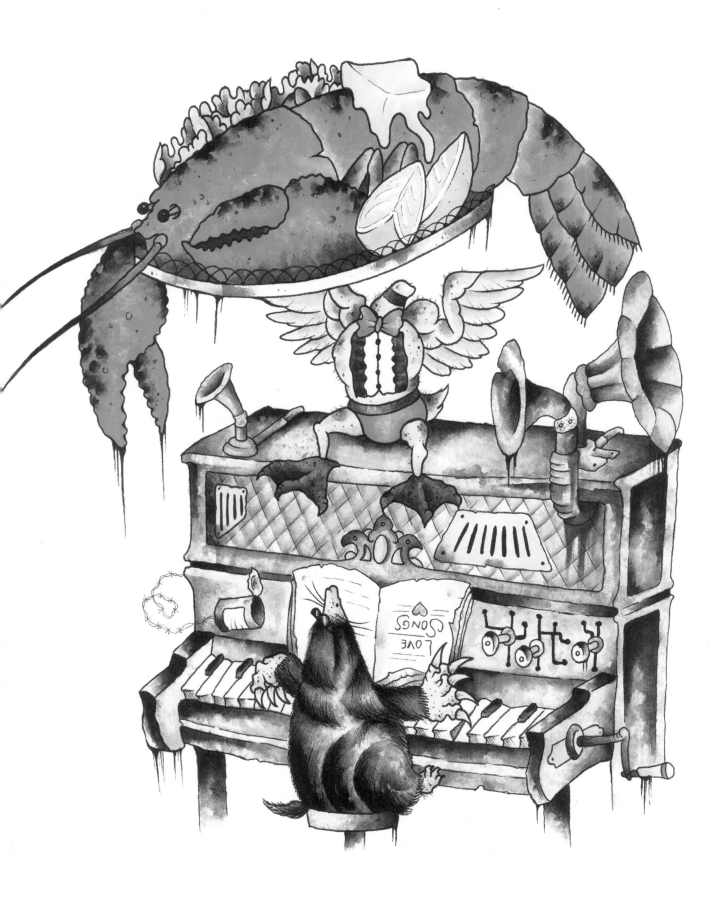

So the duckling she lifted
As he nervously shifted
For being headless can leave one quite feeble

With the purest sincerity
And a surgeons dexterity
The lady duckling produced thread and needle

hip stitch and cross stitch
She connected flesh to bone
Making sure they
Were firmly connected

he laughter and elation

That was filling their hearts

Was more glorious than the ducks

Could have expected

With a final pull and a snip
The headless duckling could barely gr[...]
It was complete, the two birds were one

He had a playmate and a buddy
Someone to swim with and get muddy
She had a lover and a comrade for fun

And so,

    Blissfully complete

      Sporting four webby feet

        The double duckling set off, quite absurd

A built in best friend to stand with till the end

The life of the world's first...

            LOVEBIRD

Tax A. Dermy

As elusive as the creatures he pursues, few details are known concerning the origins of **Mr. Taxafred Arnold Dermy**. His affinity for animals and undiscovered species are well documented, yet who he is and where he comes from is harder information to acquire.
Never far from the side of his trusted field illustrator and best friend **Merts E. Loc**, the pair has spent their lives discovering and documenting the most incredible unknown species from around the world.
He was recently quoted, "Far to many a year have I waited to release our findings to the eager minds of this world. So let it begin, with this unbelievable tale of unconditional love".
Enjoy!

Merts E. Loc

Never far from the side of his eccentric benefactor and best friend Tax, Mr. Loc is Mr. Dermy's eternal shadow, documenting their outlandish adventures and steering him from danger whenever possible.
A man of few words, little information is known of his birth place or the makings of his person.
Quiet though he may be, his ability to capture the essence and perfect likeness of the animals he witnesses is truly uncanny.
It was because of this particular skill and his rigid politeness, Merts was quickly dubbed irreplaceable to Tax, shortly after their introduction deep in the jungles of South America many years ago...
They have been inseparable ever since.

CPSIA information can be obtained
at www.ICGtesting.com
Printed in the USA
LVHW07n1918061018
592689LV00002B/3/P